Frenemies
in Space

Also by Marian Allen

Novels

SAGE Book 1: The Fall of Onagros

SAGE Book 2: Bargain With Fate

SAGE Book 3: Silver and Iron

Sideshow in the Center Ring

A Dead Guy at the Summerhouse

The Wolves of Port Novo
(Previously Published as Eel's Reverence)

Bar Sinister

Short Story Collections

Lonnie, Me and. . . .

Lonnie, Me and the Hound of Hell

Turtle Feathers

The King of Cherokee Creek

MA's Monthly Hot Flashes: 2002-2009

Other Earth, Other Stars

Shifty

Frenemies
in Space

Marian Allen

Per Bastet

Frenemies in Space
Stories Set in the World of Sideshow in the Center Ring

Published by Per Bastet Publications LLC, P.O. Box 3023 Corydon, IN 47112

Cover art by Teagan R. Geneviene

ISBN 978-1-942166-84-9

Frenemies in Space

Safe House

So of course something had to go wrong. Oscar Wilde said *No good deed goes unpunished.* Or maybe it was Mark Twain. Groucho Marx? Somebody said it, anyway, or something like it.

How would *I* know? I'm not a lit jock; I'm a star. Cornelia Phelan, known to my friends and to those who pass for my friends as Connie.

I left Earth to vacation on the planet Marner and never went back. Not because the Marneri look like humanoid cats, which is a big draw for a lot of humans, but because. . . . Well, for a lot of reasons, none of which is that they look like humanoid cats. I don't like cats. I don't like humans, either, which is two strikes against the Marneri, to begin with. In their favor they have this: they aren't, in fact, cats or humans.

So I stayed on Marner, and I established my non-profit Non-Governmental Organization, Tell It To The Empress. Seems that the Marneri have a contractual business arrangement we humans call "slavery" when it applies to somebody else and "job security" when it applies to us. It seems to suit the Marneri, but it also seems the Marneri rich-and-psychopathic are as good at abusing their legal arrangements as we are at abusing ours.

Although any "slave" can technically take refuge with any free citizen and petition the Empress for relief from an abusive contract holder, there isn't always a free citizen willing to take on the expense or responsibility.

That's where my NGO came in: I set up a string of safe houses, starting with Muimmea, the capital of Wellki. Abused

1

slaves with nowhere else to go could take refuge with me by claiming sanctuary in one of my safe houses.

The rich-and-psychopathic didn't like it.

Now, my mama and daddy might have raised a fool, but I wasn't raised by them; I was raised by my Aunt Bootsie, and "fool" was something that happened to other people. So, when the safe house in Muimmea stopped reporting asylum seekers, I knew something was wrong.

I left a voice mail with everybody I knew on Marner, telling them I was going to check out the Muimmea safe house. Something was out of kilter, which meant somebody was doing something to un-kilter things, which meant I wanted my back covered. I wasn't nervous enough to take muscle out visiting with me, but I was just barely nervous enough to want people who cared about me to know where I was planning to be. (Aunt Bootsie. No fools.)

~*~

"Nobody's coming in," the manager, a female named Boowun said, when we checked the record books in her office in the empty house. "I can't help it if nobody's coming in. Everybody's happy. That's a good thing, isn't it? Why aren't you happy?"

If I had a superpower — other than sarcasm — it would be reading body language. Boowun was lying. Her eyes were just thaaat much too wide and her ears were twitching.

Still, the accounts showed no expenditure for food, clothing, or laundry, and only routine housecleaning. In fact, she passed along a letter of complaint from Jooper, the housekeeper, offering to waive the per-room-in-use add-on she'd negotiated in return for a higher flat routine rate.

You can't ask for more positive proof of non-occupancy than that.

Much as I'd like to have thought that my safe houses had put the fear of whatever Marneri worshiped into the psychopaths, I didn't even begin to think so.

"Well, you've got a refugee now," I said.

"Who?"

"Me."

Boowun looked terrified, then shrewd, then relieved. She nodded. "All right," she said. "Good."

~*~

I called around again, chatting or leaving messages, explaining what I was up to. There was a certain amount of argument, naturally, but I'm stubborn and I'm persuasive. I promised to just spend the night and come home in the morning. They say curiosity killed the cat, but there were no cats here and I had no reason to suspect any kind of violence afoot.

Boowun and I ate a light supper of local fish and a salad, played a few rounds of Tap the Counter, all of which she won, and I closed myself into the room I'd chosen.

~*~

Time passed

~*~

I wasn't quite asleep when he slipped in through the window. One of the things you learn to do during filming is to half-doze, so you can wake up refreshed in an instant. When the window eased open and a stocky figure slid in and crouched while he waited for his eyes to adjust to the darkness, I went from drowsing to adrenalin-pumped high alert.

He duck-walked over to my pallet and put a hand over my mouth.

I rolled into my punch and connected right on the button. He fell backward with a thud and sneezed.

"Ow!" he roared. I jumped up and flipped on the light. He glared at me over the hand he held to his nose and said, "You again! What've you got against my nose?"

"Budhi?"

"Why are you so violent? I've never hurt you!" He looked at the blood on his hand. "Just in self-defense."

3

"Don't even think about it. What are you doing in my bedroom, anyway?"

"I didn't know it was you, did I? I thought it was a real person."

"Excuse me?"

"A real person." He thumped his chest. "Like me. My mistake." He snagged my sheet and mopped blood from his face, hand, and chest.

My hands itched to go for him again, but I can't fight unless I'm pissed, and curiosity had the better of me.

"Okay," I said, "pretend I'm a real person. You sneak into my bedroom and put a hand over my mouth so I can't scream. Then what?"

He stopped ruining the facility linen and stared at me.

"Not so you can't *scream*. So you can't *talk*. So you have to listen to me."

"I stand corrected. Want some tea?"

That threw him off-balance, which was my intention.

"Uh, sure. Uh, got some of that Earth stuff?"

"Always," I said. "Honey, too."

Some Marneri loved teas from Earth, some hated it. They all loved honey. While I made tea on the single burner in the room's minuscule cooking corner, I drew Budhi into idle chat, according to Marneri custom. You concentrate on the tea while you're making it and taking the first sip. You talk after that.

All the time, I was asking myself, *Listen to you say what?* Did he come to talk to some random asylum seeker, some specific one, or was he lying and he had actually come intending to talk to me?

We squatted face-to-face with our teacups on the floor between us while Budhi nearly over-brimmed his with imported honey, took our first gingerly sips, and I began.

"Who did you expect to find in this room?"

"Nobody."

"Do you *want* me to pop you again?"

He swayed to the side, but I was only threatening, not swinging.

"Nobody in particular, I mean. I saw somebody was in here, and I came in to . . . to talk to them."

"About what?"

I picked up my tea and Budhi eyed the cup apprehensively, in case I decided to pitch it at him.

"About personal responsibility," he said. "About the importance of honoring a contract. Giving your business associate what they've paid for."

I got it.

"You came to scare an asylum seeker into going back into an abusive situation."

He looked down his bloody nose at me.

"They aren't being 'abused'. They get asked to do a little extra, or they don't like the way they're talked to, or they sign on to work at one place and they're needed at another place or something like that. If they were really abused, they could go to the Exchange."

"Have you ever been a slave?"

"Sure. Have you?"

I grinned. Probably evilly, because Budhi shuffled back a few inches.

"You haven't, but I have," he said. "It was tough, sometimes, but it's not like it's forever."

"Tell you what," I said. "How about you sell yourself to me, and we'll see how uncomfortable I can make you without breaking any laws hard enough to get the Exchange involved."

He shook his head so hard, I was afraid his nose would start bleeding again.

I took a wild guess.

"You're a slave now, aren't you?"

He stirred his tea with a claw and said, not looking at me, "I had some financial difficulties. Made some bad investments."

"Who are you . . . 'working' for?"

He looked back over his shoulder at the open window.

I lowered my voice. "Do you work in pairs? Is somebody out there listening?"

He went for the window like a flash. I had forgotten how fast he was.

Damn! I'd lost him!

But, no, he actually came back in and sat down to finish his tea. "Nobody listening. I didn't think so, but it's better to be careful."

"Who are you working for?" I asked again. "Why did you come here?"

He finished his tea and licked the cup to get as much of the honey as he could.

"Why should I tell you?" he asked, as if he had something to bargain with.

"To keep me from sending my security guards after you? I hire my goons from up in the Omata hills, where men are men and women can whale the tar out of them."

"I would tell you if I could," he said quickly. "But it isn't that simple."

I put on a sympathetic face. Being a trained actress sure came in handy, sometimes.

"Poor Budhi," I said. "Looks like you've gotten yourself into trouble. Let me help you." Not above lying, I said, "I *want* to help you."

"Well. . . ."

"I'll get you some more tea."

We reverted to small talk while I made us each a second cup, ostentatiously making his as much honey as tea.

When we were facing each other again and I was drinking tea and Budhi was sipping nectar, I said, "Are you working for one person, or more than one person?"

He nearly dropped his cup.

"Mo — More. How did you know?"

"I know a lot of things," I said, sagely, having no idea what I'd just guessed. "Fill in the picture for me."

"Nobody who could make real trouble has come here, yet," he said. "Just misunderstandings, mostly, or troublemakers, or people with no real gripe who are trying to bluff their contract holders into concessions not granted by the contract."

"But," I said, as enlightenment flooded me, "if the safe houses gain credence among slaves, we might start being used by people who could make trouble for people who don't want attention paid to their business practices."

"I knew you already knew. You probably expected me. You hit me on the nose on purpose."

"I didn't! I mean, well, yes, I did, but it wasn't premeditated." Throwing honesty to the wind, I said, "Of course I expected somebody to come threaten a supposed asylum seeker, but I had no way of knowing it would be *you*."

He made the Marneri sound that's equal to a skeptical *Hmph*.

"So what now?" I asked.

"Now I go back and tell them you know what they're doing. I tell them you're going to hire security for the safe houses. I tell them they need to do a better job of watching their slaves and making sure nobody gets away from them."

So *not* what I wanted to happen!

"Or how about this," I said. "How about I call the guards I have stationed around this building —" which I didn't, "—and they haul you off to the Exchange and tell the Empress you're conspiring to flout her laws?"

"Wait, wait, wait!" He put down his tea cup with a clatter, shouting into the air to the imaginary security guards he thought were moving in on him. "I'm just a slave! I have to do what I'm told! What choice do I have?"

"What choice do you have?" I smiled sweetly and sipped my tea. "Why, you could claim sanctuary here while we tell the

Empress you're informing on a bunch of potential law-flouters at great risk to your life."

He put a hand over his stomach as if — I don't know — as if he had a panic bellyache or something.

"Or," I said, "you can go back and tell your bosses what you said you would tell them *and* I tell the Empress you informed on the them."

His mouth fell open and he began to stress-pant, eyes wide, ears flat against his head.

"Totally up to you," I said.

And that's how my personal nemesis became a member of my staff. If I gave out awards, he would win Least Trusted Employee of the Month, like, every month. But at least he's on my side.

Sort of.

The Best Years of Your Life

I can't say I always knew I'd be a star — "Connie Phelan, the Queen of TerraNet Holovision", as the entertainment broadcasts call me. I can't even say I had any particular ambition. I just grew up feeling like a wolf in a world of sheep in armor — sheep who walked around saying, "Mmmmm, I taste sooo goood. Wouldn't it be wonderful to rip into some of these succulent muscles? But you can't. You're just not good enough."

That's what it was like, growing up in an alley behind a high-priced condo.

The only weapons I had to fight that feeling were a quick wit and a smart mouth, so that's what I used. My Aunt Bootsie caught me more than once, skipping school to stand on a downtown street corner, telling jokes and tossing out insult humor with a chalk circle in front of me for tips.

When I look back now, I'm sorry I gave Aunt Bootsie so much trouble, especially when I can remember how grateful I was to her for taking me away from my worthless folks and raising me with love and actual adult supervision.

"Enjoy these years while you're in 'em," Aunt Bootsie said, when we got home after a silent ride into her shabbily respectable neighborhood. "Your high school years are the best years of your life."

"God, I hope not," I said, pulling my head back to avoid the face-tap I knew was coming.

"Don't blaspheme," she said, the caution weak from overuse. "Connie, Connie, what am I gonna do with you?"

I shrugged, sullen with shame and resentment, blaming the world for getting me in trouble with my aunt.

~*~

A new kid, Benton DeHaven, a trumpet whiz, transferred to my school, Day High, from Who-Remembers-Where, recruited by our band director. The history teachers tell me schools used to be all about contact sports, until the safety regulations passed to protect kids got so tough that school sports were eliminated. Then everything was about who had the best band.

It didn't take long for the new guy to be targeted by Ainsley Torrington III, our resident bully that year. Sounds like the name of a delicate flower, but Ainsley was a beef-fed mountain in designer clothes.

See, it was supposed to be good for young people to fraternize, rather than to learn through electronics. It was supposed to improve our social skills. And it was fashionable for rich people to send their offspring to public schools for a couple of years "to pick up the common touch," so they could understand the people who would be working for them some day. Since everybody knew for certain the rich kids would grow up to be bosses, the rich kids generally bossed everybody around in school. Preparation for later life, I guess.

Benton DeHaven's parents were fairly well off, but still not quite out of public school status. Right up there at the top, but not quite out. Middle-management material, everybody figured him for.

Me, I didn't care who was going to be important some day, because I intended to be important, myself. As for physical threats, I'd been knocked around enough at home to know how to duck, roll with the punches, and heal, depending on how good any particular bully's aim was from one encounter to the next. Besides, bullies don't like being laughed at any more than anybody else, and I was pretty good at raising laughs. So bullies and I left each other alone. Mostly.

Anyway, I was nearby when Ainsley and his crew caught Benton outside the band room one day.

"You play trumpet, huh?" Ainsley had a voice I was studying for comic effect, because I'd never heard anything like it before. Dumb jock posh, I'd say it was. I had done a few jokes in it on the street corner, with some good response. Response I could spend, which was my major aim.

Benton hefted his instrument case and said, "Trumpet. Yes."

I could have said the words along with Ainsley: "Blow me."

Oh, how funny Ainsley's crew thought that was! Benton blushed crimson from his hairline to at least his neckline, and that made them laugh so hard, he was able to walk away.

"The Carnival of Venice" was Benton's showpiece, and the poor mutt had to play it at every school assembly. Sometimes I think they scheduled assemblies just so they could show off how good he was at "Carnival of Venice".

Naturally, I started calling Day High *the Carnival of Dumbass*. Every time Benton played his piece, I would say, "Oh, listen! Our school song!" Everybody who knew my joke would laugh, and of course the in-joke spread until the whole school snickered whenever the music got introduced.

~*~

I came back from one of my afternoons playing hooky to find Benton with two black eyes and a swollen nose.

Ainsley and his crew went around making loud noise about their defense of school honor.

"Pencil-necked geek thinks he's funny, calling our school stupid," Ainsley said, and his buddies chimed in with their agreement. I guess that's what they were mumbling; they were bobbing their heads like a flock of dancing parrots.

I said, "He's playing Carnival of Venice. It's just a song about some party in some town in some country. It doesn't have anything to do with our school."

"He made it about our school. Comes in from some stupid other school and calls our school stupid."

I crowded into his personal space. "*I* made the joke, Ainsley, *I* did. Me. I, who stand now before you. Not Benton, not whoever it is who wrote that goofy song they make Benton play. *I'm* the one who calls that song and this school Carnival of Dumbass. Guess why."

You might think I was flirting with danger, but there you'd be wrong. Like I said, I was always locked and loaded with insults, and I wasn't afraid to use them. Since Ainsley would have to grow up, rise through the ranks of his mother's business, and hire somebody to think of a comeback for anything I said to him during the best years of his life, he generally tried to stay on my good side.

Now he just sneered at me. His friends gave that sly, throaty, haw-haw chuckle that means their team scored a good one on somebody — it didn't matter that their team hadn't scored anything but a pie in the face, the chuckle itself made them feel like they won.

There's no help for stupid. Stupid's lucky, because it's too stupid to know that.

~*~

In the school lunch line, I entered the code for rare steak and raw eggs into the food printer and pulled out a plate of medium steak and over-easy eggs, along with an edible note warning against consuming undercooked food. Never mind that it wasn't real steak or real eggs. I'm sighing and shaking my head, here.

Benton looked up as I slid into the seat across from him. He dodged his head sideways before he saw it was me.

"Get away," he said, all stuffed up with the Knuckle Sandwich Flu. "I only hab two eyes and wud doze. I do't eved dnow you. Why are you doi'g this to be?"

"I'm not doing anything to you." Inside, part of me was saying, *He's right. You did this to him.* Another part was jumping up and down with its fingers in its ears, yelling, *La, la, la, I can't hear you.* "Why didn't you duck? He doesn't just telegraph his punches, he sends them by pony express.

You should have seen that punch coming hours ahead of time."

"I could see he was thi'king about sobthi'g—"

"It *is* so rare, it stands out."

He seemed to give up on not talking to me, maybe because he was intelligent enough to realize that not knowing me hadn't been much of a defense. "I wish I dever had to play Cardival of Vedice agaid. I was sick of it, eved before this. At least I won't have to play it u'til by dose heals."

"So why didn't you taze him?"

"I do't carry a weapod."

"I don't carry a weapon in school because I can't afford a license. Ainsley doesn't carry a weapon in school because he's a serial offender. I think you could get one pretty easy."

"I do't carry a weapod. I could, but I do't."

I stopped cutting my steak. "You don't? Deliberately? What are you, some kind of Amish or something?"

"I do't believe id it. 'Ad eye for ad eye bakes both half-bli'd.' What if dobody went arbed?"

"Then everybody but Ainsley and his crew would have noses the size of their heads and eyes like raccoons."

"Be the chadge you want to see id the world," Benton said.

High school is like that.

~*~

It barely skimmed the surface of my vast well of sarcasm for me to turn Ainsley's attack on Benton into something Ainsley would never forget. Or so I thought.

I found out differently at our ten-year class reunion.

Sure, I went. I was rich and famous by then, a big star and still rising. I wanted to revel in my status, but I soon found out that reunions are just high school with a cash bar.

Ainsley was now a CEO (not of TerraNet, happily for me). His old crew either worked directly under him or for allied companies. Benton worked for him, too. Middle management.

13

Ainsley and his crew ignored me so completely, I was satisfied he remembered me with excellent clarity.

When I bumped into Benton at the bar, where he was fetching a drink for Ainsley, he smiled and nodded with a vague friendliness.

"Congratulations on your success," he said, as if my rhubarb had won a blue ribbon at the county fair. "I always wondered where entertainers came from."

"Same place suck-ups come from," I said. "Dear old Day High."

There were four bartenders, and Benton and I put in our orders at the same time. While we waited, he turned to me again. Some people never learn.

"What's it like, spending your life letting other people laugh at you?"

"I don't know," I said. "Why don't you tell me?"

His lips thinned and that full-head flush of his washed over him. "That was uncalled for."

The conscience my Aunt Bootsie had labored so hard to wake up in me woke up a little.

"It really was," I said, as we picked up our drinks. "I'm sorry."

I followed him back to Ainsley, curious to see how he was treated.

Ainsley took the drink and threw an arm around Benton's shoulder. "Thanks, Carn." Arm still fixing Benton in place, Ainsley asked the crowd around them, "Know why I call him Carn? It's short for Carnival of Dumbass. That was what I called him in high school 'cause he played this dumbass song all the time on the trumpet or something." Everybody laughed, including Benton.

Ainsley took a swig of his drink, obviously not his first of the evening. "High school," he said, maudlin nostalgia — or maybe one too many — misting his eyes. "Best years of our

14

lives." He gave Benton a little shake and released him. "Right, Carn? Best years of our lives, eh?"

"Yes," said Benton, and I believed he meant it, God help him. "Yes, they were."

Dressed By Design

It's a good thing I'm a man who's comfortable in his skin, because I'm considered as much of an oddball here on Marner as I was on Earth.

My mother used to tell me about the time she took me clothes shopping when I was two, and all I wanted to look at were girls' clothes. She scanned the tag of the one I liked best and projected a hologram of me, wearing it, and I roared and tried to punch the hologram. I didn't want to *wear* it!

She took me to the doctor to explore my gender options, and he said what I already knew at two: I didn't feel female, and I didn't want to dress like one. I just loved their clothes and the way their clothes looked on them.

That seems to strike everybody in the universe as weird, but that's me, and that's the baseline for how I grew up to be "Jackie Eastman, Designer to the Stars."

When I first opened my new venture on Marner, an increasingly popular upscale tourist destination and tax haven, I couldn't get anybody to work for me. Everybody thought I must be crazy, for one thing.

The humans who live on Marner are short on disposable income, since they put most of their profits back into their own start-ups and off-Earth branches. The tourists bring their own clothes, and don't want to pick up more to ship back.

As for the native Marneri, although they're humanoid, Marneri are covered with fur. They don't wear clothes. Most of them don't. There are a few who shave their entire bodies except for their heads and dress like humans. The other Marneri call them "shavetails" and despise them. The humans they hang

17

around with don't think much of them, either. Also, they tend to buy off the rack.

I might be crazy, but I'm not stupid. I planned to start with a line of accessories, which Marneri do wear, in a wide range of prices: fur clips, belts, purses, necklaces, bracelets, ankle-bracelets, and earrings. Then I'd go into scarves, shawls, ponchos, rain wear, and then I'd be into clothing suitable for the fashionably furred.

It was easy enough to find artisans for my first phase, since accessories were already common. Phase two wouldn't be difficult in production, either, since Marneri do have blankets, tablecloths, and curtains; the difficulty would be in persuading them it was respectable to put fabric on their *bodies*.

I wanted the staff to reflect the clientèle I planned to attract, which meant I wanted mostly Marneri for office and sales. Marneri didn't want to work for me, for obvious reasons.

After months of doing my own buying, hiring, advertising, letter-writing, and supervising, as well as long-distance managing my Earth business, I finally got an answer to all my Help Wanted ads and feelers: Eppy.

You know how Marneri look kind of like human cats to us? Eppy looked especially like one. Her muzzle was more pronounced than most Marneri's and her ears were higher up the sides of her head. Her matte brown fur tumbled in medium-long corkscrew curls, and she had bedecked herself in bargain-bin glittery clips along her shoulders.

She came in giggling, and she giggled throughout the interview, which we conducted in Tudolinguo, a trade language developed to make communication easier. She kept her eyes narrowed and avoided looking me in the face. Every so often, she rubbed the side of her muzzle with the back of her hand. My wife, who is much better than I am at reading Marneri body language, had pointed out behavior like that before, and told me it indicated nervousness.

It got worse when we got to prior employment questions.

She had worked in her grand-sire's noodle store, growing up and through school.

"And then?"

Giggle. Fidget. Fidget.

I waited.

Finally, she looked at me, as if she had given up hope that she would get the job.

"I worked at Bellington Import/Export."

There were a lot of import/export businesses on Marner. I had never heard of this one. Probably a small family one, just big enough to hire a local or two.

I still didn't say anything. My wife tells me that keeping your mouth shut makes other people open theirs. She should know, since the only time she keeps her mouth shut is when she's gritting her teeth in rage, and she does that most of the time. Doesn't suffer fools, my wife.

Eppy took a deep breath and said, "I got fired. I was supposed to unpack and log in arrivals." Defensively, she said, "And I did!" She looked away again. "But I spent too much time with some things. I didn't work fast enough."

"What did you spend so much time with?"

Fidget.

"Clothes."

I stopped thinking about how I was going to end this with as little embarrassment as possible.

She blinked, her thin pink lips turned down. "I know it's abnormal. The humans made fun of me. Dangled laces in front of me and told me to play. The Marneri were *furious* at me for giving the humans another reason to act like we're walking, talking pets."

"Clothes?" I said.

She looked at me again. "I love them! I don't want to—" she wrinkled her nose, "—*wear* any, but I love them. I love the way they look and the way they fold and hang. I love the way the parts fit together."

"I understand," I said. "I do understand."

The unnatural grimace on her face melted and her ears relaxed from their drawn-back attitude.

"You do?"

"I feel the same way."

She giggled again and then started to cry. It took about half an hour and two cups of herbal tea before she could read and sign the necessary paperwork.

~*~

On her first full day, Eppy came in with extra fur clips on her shoulders and the sides of her head, waving her unfolded eNews sheet.

"Did you see this? All the females are celebrating! You ought to make something to commemorate this!"

She put the sheet on my desk and touched one of the headlines. The story expanded to fill the sheet. She touched the Translate button and selected Tudolinguo.

BERRA INDUCTED INTO CHEEKAH FLYING CORPS

Cheekah was the Division of Marner where my office was.

"This seems to be a big deal," I said.

"A big deal?!" Eppy proceeded to bring me up to speed.

It seems that females, revered as the source of life, were under extreme social pressure to avoid hazardous jobs. This Berra had defied the pressure and enrolled as a military pilot. There was no law against it, and she had excelled, to the delight of other Marneri females with socially transgressing ambitions. Like ones who loved clothes, for instance.

I took Eppy's advice and commissioned a line of jewelry, belts, purses, and haversacks featuring the first letter of Berra's name in Standard Earth and in Marneri script. I wanted to put wings on them, but they don't have birds on Marner, so we left those off.

They sold hand over fist. I even took the plunge and put out a line of scarves with the same device printed on it, using the Cheekah Flying Corps colors.

These also sold, although Eppy told me the Marneri hung the scarves on their walls or flew them like banners from poles. I coaxed her to let me tie one around her neck, just to show her how it was done, but she pulled it off as soon as I nodded satisfaction with the look.

~*~

Eppy quickly went from bringing me ideas to sketching possible designs. When I offered to teach her to construct clothing, fitting it on dress forms, I was afraid she'd hyperventilate with delight.

The House of Eastman on Marneri had so little call for clothing, we made what outfits were ordered ourselves. Eppy had plenty of time to learn, beginning with small, simple pieces and working her way up to large, deceptively simple-looking ensembles.

She never even held any clothing up to see, in a mirror, how it would look on her, but she stopped wearing cheap fur clips and bought her accessories (at cost) exclusively from our House.

Before we knew it, five years had passed, and Eppy was indispensable. When my wife suggested I make Eppy a partner, I was ashamed to admit to myself that I hadn't considered it because I needed her as she was.

You can imagine how relieved I was when I asked her if she wanted to be a partner in the Marner enterprise, and she said, "I thought I already *was* a partner."

I doubled her salary, and nothing else changed. I taught her tailoring, and she taught me what the Marneri might actually wear. More and more Marneri adopted various articles of clothing (not including Eppy), and the business grew.

Because she associated that first commemorative line she had suggested to me with the first female Flying Corps inductee, Eppy followed the career of Flight Commander Berra and kept me updated.

"Berra dedicated a new plane."

"Here's a good interview with Berra. She talks about the importance of the Flight Corps in keeping peace."

"Berra delivered an address to the United Divisions Conference."

"Berra got another honorary medal."

At some point, I asked, "Does Berra ever do anything that isn't just ceremonial?"

"What do you mean?"

"Does she do regular pilot stuff, do you think? Does she, you know, fly for the corps?"

"Fly missions?"

"Yeah."

Eppy blinked at me. "Oh, no! She's much too valuable for that!"

~*~

One day, in the Marneri season we Earthlings called Spring, Eppy came in and closed the door behind her.

That was a wonder. She loves the interoffice phone so much I'm always surprised she doesn't use it when I'm standing right there next to her.

"What's up?" I kept my voice low, since she was flapping a hand at me to signal quiet, her gilded nails flashing in the light.

"It's her," she hissed. "It's Berra."

"What does she want?" I asked. In all the pictures Eppy had shown me, Berra wore nothing but her own fur and a sash-of-rank pinned with medals signifying achievements. Even on non-military occasions, when she was more or less a civilian, she wore little more than a few simple fur clips.

"She says she wants *clothes*! A special outfit."

"She getting married again?" I was ashamed of myself the minute I said it. It made Eppy laugh, which made me feel even worse. I try not to be mean; being mean and getting rewarded for it is just wrong.

It was a cheap joke, too. Berra had been, as they said in the gossip articles, unlucky in love. She had formed a mating pair three times, had dissolved the pairing every time before a year was up, and hadn't generated kits once. Her exes had walked away with apparently bruised hearts and egos, not to mention big chunks of her military pay.

"Show her in."

I'm not anywhere near as good as my wife is at reading Marneri facial and body cues, but even I could tell Berra was a woman on a mission. Her lips were parted and stretched and her eyes were narrowed in a smile. She gave me a firm handshake, showing she was familiar with Earth courtesy. I had gotten reconciled to licking noses, which was the Marneri way, but I never did like it, so I appreciated her cultural sensitivity. That was the military PR people at work, I guess.

"Sit down," I said. "What can I do for you?"

"I'm told you're a blunt man. Is that true?"

How was I supposed to answer that? Usually, if somebody says, "I'm blunt," what they mean is, "I'm rude." I shrugged and said, "I don't mince words."

She nodded. "That's good. I hope you don't mind if I speak plainly, too. I've spent the past few years of my life watching everything I say, publicly and privately, and I'm *tired* of it."

The emphasis she put on the word *tired* said more than language ever could.

She went on, "I might as well begin by telling you that I've never approved of clothing for Marneri. It's silly. If the Divine Empress had meant us to wear clothes, she wouldn't have given us fur."

"It's a point," I admitted.

"But there's something about special clothing for special events. It seems to add to the importance of the function. It seems to make people feel more in tune with what's happening, more a part of it. It seems to be a sort of gift they give to themselves and a tribute they pay to the occasion."

"That's very well put." I scribbled it down. "Mind if I use that in an ad?"

"Just don't quote me," she said.

I wrote *Anonymous* after the quote and nodded.

"I have a special occasion coming up, and I've decided I want something very special to wear. Something that suits me in particular. I don't know what you charge for a personal design, but tell me and I'll make sure to have the funds available."

"If I can claim you as a client," I said, "I can give you a nice discount."

She shook her head. "I'm not allowed to do endorsements of any kind, and I believe that would count as an endorsement."

Well, of course, that was the idea, but I understood that the military didn't want to get into the business of boosting a fashion designer.

"We'll negotiate the price," I said.

"I'll be flying my personal plane to this event," she said, "so the clothing has to be something I can fly in. It has to leave my arms free. It shouldn't be elaborate, but I want it to be beautiful."

Eppy took her measurements and I questioned her and showed her fabric samples, matching them against her fur.

Unlike Eppy's, Berra's fur was short, a soft blue-gray with a white patch just below her throat. By the time she left, I had a concept sketch for her. She initialed it, and Eppy and I went to work.

I would have liked to put her in red, but she vetoed that as too flashy, so we chose a coarse silk fabric with a dull gold background and a curling abstract pattern in thin black, thick white, and a silver that had a blue cast to it and almost looked like transparency showing the fur beneath. It had a high neck with a triangle cut out, leaving the white patch below her throat exposed. A black pearl pendant hung from the collar to the exact center of the white patch. The full, roomy sleeves fastened at her wrists with gold cufflinks stamped with her military insignia, and the simple black trousers buttoned at her ankles. She balked at new shoes, preferring to wear her flying boots. It spoiled the effect, I thought, but she was the customer, so boots it was.

At the final fitting, she stood in front of the mirror for a long time — my ladies often do that. She stroked the cloth covering her arms.

"How does it feel?"

"Perfect."

"Suitable for the occasion?" She never had told us what it was.

"Perfect. It's just what I had hoped: beautiful, dignified, luxurious, simple. I feel strong in it. I feel . . . happy."

That was funny, because she didn't look happy. Determined and ready to be satisfied about something, yes, but not what I would call happy. Of course, as I said, I'm no expert in reading Marneri body language.

That was the last time I saw her. It was two days later when Eppy showed me the eNews.

"Why?" Eppy asked the question. "Why would a flying ace suddenly crash into a mountain? Do you think it was sabotage? One of those old cranks who don't want females to do anything but bear kits?"

Nobody ever knew for sure. There was a rumor that she had never generated kits because she was sterile, and she found out and crashed her plane. There was a rumor that she had a terminal illness. There was a rumor that she had sold military

25

secrets to a foreign power, although what military secrets a publicity figure would have is anybody's guess. There was a rumor she was being blackmailed, and a million rumors as to what the blackmail material was.

Me, I think she worked her butt off breaking a barrier and becoming what she was born wanting to be, and then she wasn't allowed to do it. I think it poisoned every crack and corner of her adult life, and I think she didn't see any end to it. I think she saw flying into a mountain as the most special occasion she'd ever attended or would ever attend — a defiant celebration of herself.

I could be wrong.

The Woman Who Wasn't a Shave-Tail

I was standing here, right in this very spot, when this bare-necked beggar, not old but not a kit, came up. He was yellow-orange — they're never anything but trouble — and obviously out of place in the big city. You know how these yokels are . . . well, I guess you don't, you being an off-worlder. They're either rough-looking or over-groomed; some of them use pomade to get that fur just so, you know? This fella was a little on the shaggy side. Nothing on — not a chestpack, not a purse-belt, nothing. Oh — he had a burlap pocket fastened to his fur with a couple of pinch-clips; it was up under his arm, where the hicks like to tuck them. Those evil city-slickers can't steal your alfalfa money if you clip it right up there under your arm, right?

"Go on, get out of here," I said. "You're blocking the table."

He looked around, but nobody was interested in jewelry and holy trinkets; this stuff I put outside usually grabs tourists, but this was off-season. He pulled out his pink slip — his status papers — to show me he was freehold — like I couldn't tell from his neck: no collar, you know? — as of the Release.

See, at the Release — comes every seven years — all slaves are freed. All slave records automatically roll over to freehold at the Central Registry.

—You're doing that face: that "slavery is evil" face you Terrans make. Excuse me, I don't mean to be rude, but it gets my back hairs up. Look at this — look at how they're standing on end back there. I hate that.

Our slaves get a signing fee — sometimes pretty hefty — in place of a salary. They have a union. No kidnapping allowed, like you people used to do. — Okay, okay, it was before your time. No offense meant, none taken, I hope. —Every seven years, they're all freed and either sign up again or don't.

"So you're free," I said to the beggar. "Congratulations."

"I need a place to spend the night, and some food."

"Why tell me? Look—" I pointed across the street. "There's a man with a brazier. Smell that spiced meat? He sells that to hungry people. And look over there — There's a sign in that window, 'Rooms to Let'."

"I don't have any money."

"Is that my problem?"

"Help me. Please." He held out his palms, like this, with the fingers spread. That's like a kit wanting to be picked up, it's that kind of asking. He was telling me he wasn't a man compared to me, that his universe revolved around me.

His palms were calloused but not cracked. He had done plenty of hard work on a long-term basis; had kept his pads medicated until they toughened up, a sure sign of a good worker. So what was he doing in the city, asking me for a handout?

Luck. I'm a very lucky fella. Oh, yes.

"Get out of here! All right, here's some money. Go away."

He clutched the coins and said, "Thank you." I expected him to give me a grin and go try the act on somebody else, but he just stood there.

"No more," I said. "Move along, or I'll call the law."

He flashed a bitter look and said, "That's all the law is good for: rousting people who need help, but never helping them."

"So what do you want?" I had to ask, right? "You need money, go sell yourself. I notice your old master didn't re-negotiate for you."

"I'm in trouble. Well, I'm not in trouble, but. . . . I need help."

I didn't want to hear his sad story, but I could see he was going to tell it to me. Some people, you know you aren't going to get rid of so easy. I have a nephew like that. "Here," I said. "At least come in out of the way."

He followed me into the shop, which was almost as bright as the street. When your stock in trade is shiny stuff, it pays to have plenty of light on it. Back of the counter and behind a curtain, I keep a little room with a cot and a kettle.

He sank onto the floor like he'd been on his feet since his eyes opened. I gave him a mug of sweet cha and bag of dried fruit.

"Are you happy now?" I asked.

He shook his head.

"And you're going to tell me why."

"I'm from a village a little way upstream." (He meant up the Tammi, that river on the west side of town. Goes into the back country.) He stopped to stuff a cube of dried fruit into his mouth, then I had to wait while he tried to work his teeth out of the sticky mess without drooling all over himself.

When his mouth was clear enough, he gargled, "My name is Raj."

"Shahtsi," I said. We gave each other's noses perfunctory licks. His tongue left a trail of fruit sugar that dried and itched.

He went back to his story. "My youngest brother, Jimi, left home six months ago to come here, to Muimmea, to enter the Yolanbayt."

A Yolanbayt is like what you would call a monastery. My nephew used to be in one; he's a very holy fella, but he got bored or something, and came out.

"He never got there. When we didn't hear from him, we wrote to the Yolanbayt, but they hadn't seen him. We thought a rogue slaver might have waylaid him and taken his papers, bribed a Registrar to register him slave; but we weren't too worried about it, since it was nearly the Release. Father thought it might even do him good to see the rough side of the world for a few weeks. But the Release is past, and he still hasn't shown up."

He opened his pocket and took out a small strip of paper.

"Mother sent me this in a letter. Mother's the best cook in our village. Naturally, she was put in charge of the feast. It was supposed to start on the night of the Release and go on for fifty days. Everybody who was freed was supposed to come home for part of the celebration."

"I'm just assuming that all this has something to do with what you started to tell me."

He nodded and licked fruit gum off his fingers. "Mother opened a case of dried noodles a couple of weeks before the celebration — she wanted to make sure she hadn't been shorted — and she found this."

He handed me the slip of paper. I put on my spectacles and read it.

Help. Prisoner, it said, in a kit-like scrawl. It was signed Jimi.

"He knew Mother was the festival cook," Raj said. "He managed to sneak that paper into the case that was set aside for our village, to let her know where he was. Since he hasn't come home, he must still be there."

I put my spectacles away, using that as a cover for cleaning the dried fruit paste off my nose. "Your mother told her local Registrar?"

Raj nodded. "The Registrar said she'd make an inquiry. A few days later, she said she'd heard from the factory: Jimi wasn't there."

"And you don't believe it."

"Neither does my mother. She says the Registrar doesn't believe it, either, but the Central Registry stands and falls on its paperwork, and there are no papers on a young slave named Jimi at that noodle factory."

"Well, there wouldn't be, would there, if they were keeping chained bodies?"

Chained bodies. That's pretty close to what you people used to do to each other. I'm sorry, but is it true, or isn't it? Highly illegal here, very big trouble if you're caught. If this factory was running chained bodies, they'd go as far as they had to to keep the secret.

"I can't push the law any harder," Raj said, "or the factory people might. . . . Jimi might. . . ."

I put a hand on his shoulder. "Let me call my nephew. He's a pretty smart fella."

~*~

Well, I should have known. The minute I looked up and saw that orange bumpkin blocking the sunlight, I should have known this whole thing was going to turn strange. Because my nephew came to the shop — Oh, yes, you can always count on Tosun to answer a call for help — but he had to bring her with him. Connie Phelan. I like Connie — don't get me wrong, Connie and I are like two kits in a kindle, but you never know what she'll decide to do.

"Hiya, Shahtsi," she says to me, with that big black-lipped grin of hers. Yeah, THE Connie Phelan. The Terran holo star. She lives here, on Marner. Yeah, she really looks like that. Accident with a cosmetic product, she said: patches of different colored skin and hair — black, tan, white. . . . When I first saw her, I thought she was a shave-tail.

—A shave-tail is one of us with the fur trimmed real close. Shave-tails hang around with Terrans and wear clothes. We don't think much of them, generally speaking.

So Tosun walks in with her behind him. My nephew is a good-looking fella, gray with black stripes, like me. You know how she looks — calico plus. She was wearing a black leather jumpsuit with the legs stopping just above her knees, black leather ruffles around the neck and wrists. She had diamond buckles on the toes of her black patent half-boots, and those gloves with the fingers cut out, also in black leather.

Tosun and I licked noses. Connie wiggled her multi-colored fingers at me.

Raj glanced from me to him to her and curled his lip. "I thought you said he was smart."

"I heard that." Connie showed him what his sneer might look like if it ate its vegetables and grew up big and strong. "If this half-grown rube calls me a shave-tail, I'm going to comb the hayseeds out of his hair with his teeth."

Tosun smiled reassuringly at Raj. "She's a Terran," he said. "She's a very nice person, really."

Connie snorted and sat on the cot. Probably afraid she'd get her clothes dirty, sitting on the floor with the rest of us.

"Aren't you working?" I asked. (—You watch her show? That's filmed right here in Muimmea.)

"Season hiatus. Why, Shahtsi?" She grinned again and said, "Think this would go better without me?"

"It would probably go safer without you."

"Uncle Shahtsi. . . ." Tosun thinks Connie is an Untutored Sage — a natural wise person. Natural wise mouth, maybe.

I sighed. "All right. Okay."

While I poured steaming mugs of cha for us all, Raj told them his story.

When he finished, Connie asked, "Where is this noodle factory?"

"Up Tammi River," Raj said, "past the Tammi Resort."

Tosun frowned. "Beyond Omata country. A kit would never make it home from there, even if he could escape."

Raj thumped his fist on the floor. "I have to get him out. I'll get some money. I'll buy some weapons. . . ."

My nephew shook his head. "Committing crimes of your own will only hurt your legal position. You would probably fail, and your attempt could be very dangerous for your brother."

"I have to get him out!" Raj repeated.

"We," said Connie, "have to get them all out."

"We?" I said. "All?"

"All the chained bodies. All of them."

See what I mean about her?

~*~

Tosun's mate, Tiph, was busy with their kits, an occupation of the deepest reverence, but she did some research for us. Connie's mate was off-planet on some kind of business, or he'd have been in the thick of it, too. Connie rented a sailing boat for us — a yacht or a ketch or something. It was a boat. With a sail. She offered to pay me to close up shop for as long as this took; I didn't accept the money, but she offered.

So the four of us sailed up the Tammi to a bed-and-breakfast in Domba, this one-aazzi factory town where the noodles came from. We stopped at Tammi Resort along the way: Connie and Tosun know a couple of Registrars there.

Connie left the rest of us on the boat and came back with three pink slips and three very fancy neckbands. They all matched: silver mesh, with sapphires and pearls hanging from the lower edges. She plunked them down on the mess table, where we were all gathered for a council of war, like they were barbed wire and cockle-burrs.

"Robh and Bulfa say the Registrar in Domba is a rotten, graft-grabbing, underhanded sleaze bucket. Just the type who'd fudge papers and lie through his fangs. Nothing easier than to give Jimi another name, change his age a little, let the papers roll over to freehold, and claim he'd re-upped along with the rest of the happy workers. Ask me why."

"Why?" Tosun asked. He's very good-natured.

"Because, according to Tiph, the Star-Grain Noodle Company has a very thin profit margin, and it's getting thinner."

"This was a bad year for grain," Raj told us. "The sixth in a series of bad years, but this was the worst."

I cleared my throat pointedly. "If you're through with the farm report, could she go on?"

Raj ducked his head like he'd been hit. Country-bred: Tough body, thin skin.

"So," Connie continued, "I figure the factory's owner, Yoshe Scertz, shaved some expenses by buying slaves that fell off the back of a truck, if you know what I mean. Contraband. Stolen. The paperwork shows respectable signing fees, but she really just slipped the Registrar some graft and kept the money, but claims it as a business expense when the Empress' tax collectors ask for documentation. It's a small factory — just twelve workers — but twelve signing fees add up."

She leaned forward and directed a question to me. "Say your business depended on slave labor. Say your business wasn't doing so well. Now, say all your slaves were going to be freed, and you'd have to re-negotiate for them or buy new ones, with new signing fees going to each one. What would you do?"

"Sell before the freedom came," I said. "Naturally."

"Yoshe Scertz didn't. Didn't even try."

"She was afraid the slaves would tell the buyer what she'd done," Tosun guessed.

"Wouldn't that be nice?" Connie's smile twisted sardonically. "You have such a sweet clean mind. Sometimes I envy you."

"What — what do you think she's doing?" Raj had barely met Connie, but he already knew that asking what she thought was something you hesitate to do. Trainable.

"Well, first, she paid her crooked Registrar to do the fake roll-overs, then she recorded paying generous re-up fees. I'd be willing to bet she claimed all her slaves re-signed. She's looking decent on paper, but she doesn't have much profit left."

"Just a pocket full of cash she slipped out the back door," I said.

34

Connie nodded. "A perfect time for a devastating accidental fire, leaving no survivors."

Raj grasped at the table, his claws making faint scratches in its rough surface. "She would . . . burn my brother?"

"And the others. Then she takes her secret cash, takes the Empress' loss-of-livelihood bounty, and opens another business elsewhere."

"And the Registrar?" Tosun asked.

"Maybe he'd be happy with what he's got, just sit tight and wait for another scam to come along. Maybe he'd threaten to turn her in if she didn't keep paying. Or maybe she'd arrange for him to be inspecting the work environment when the fire broke out. Another tragic victim."

Raj edged away from Connie, looking at her out of the corners of his eyes. "How did you ever think of all that?"

Tosun smiled. "Only the brightest spirit can illuminate the darkest corners of the heart."

"Whatever," said Connie. "We go in, and we buy the woman out. With my money, of course. Safe and easy."

"But she can't afford to let chained bodies pass into somebody else's hands," I said.

"She can, if she thinks she's selling to somebody as low-down as she is. So that's what she has to think."

We all looked at Connie.

"What?" she asked.

~*~

Before we left the ship, she glued this stuff on her face — she learned how to do it from her make-up artist — made her look like a shave-tail with a muzzle job: Not quite Terran, not quite Marneri.

We met in the mess again, again with the slave-collars glittering on the table.

"How do I look?" she asked.

"Disgusting," I told her. "I can hardly stand the sight of you."

35

"Perfect!"

"So you're a wealthy shave-tail and we're your slaves. Can we do this and go home?"

"Well, actually. . . ." Connie picked invisible lint off her crimson blouse. "I can't get too close to her, or she might spot the fakery." She handed a fancy collar to Tosun, and another to Raj. The third, she picked up and fastened around her own neck. "Besides, you're the businessman, O Master."

~*~

I booked all the available rooms at the River View Bed-and-Breakfast in Domba. I would have booked the whole place, but there was a honeymooning couple in the Love-Retreat Suite. Tosun got all misty-eyed over it, but I prayed to the Mother that they'd keep themselves to themselves.

The desk clerk wanted to make trouble over Connie — no shave-tails allowed — but she just stuck her muzzle in the air and let me handle it. That was probably the hardest part of the whole episode for her — keeping her mouth shut.

"You have a problem with one of my slaves?" I asked, very cold, as if he didn't have the right to breathe my air, let alone question my taste.

"We don't cater to them," he snipped.

"She isn't booking the rooms. I am. Tell me, Kit," (and I meant that to sting), "do you own this place?"

"No."

"Suppose you call the owner and say you just lost the chance to fill the place because—"

"All right, you made your point. But she has to use the back door."

"I've used the back door in better joints than this," Connie muttered.

We pretended not to hear.

"What brings you to Domba?" The clerk used that phony voice that tells you he doesn't care, and you could say, "I came to blow the place to the twelve ends of Paradise," and he'd say,

"Have a nice day."

"I'm looking for an out-of-the-way investment. Some place I can park some cash until it cools off, then pull it out again." I leaned closer. "Strictly legal, understand?"

He looked tickled furless to be on intimate terms with a wheeler-dealer like me.

"You look like a very smart fella," I said. "If you hear about a deal like that — and price is not a problem — you let me know. There'd be a finder's fee in it for you."

I peeled off one of the credit vouchers Connie had given me and slid it across the registration counter.

"I'll keep it in mind," the clerk said. "I surely will."

~*~

It wasn't quite dark when the visiphone tinkled in my room. We were all there, of course, playing cards to pass the time.

The caller was a taffy-colored fella with white hands and a white blaze on his chest.

"Welcome to our humble village," he said, with a Muimmea accent that was too perfect to be real. "I have the privilege to be the Registrar in this district. My name is Chee Tamarie. I hope I can be of service to you while you're here."

"I fail to see how," I said, "but thank you for the offer." I reached out, like I was about to turn off the 'phone.

"One moment, please!" He held up a hand, as if he could block me from the controls. "I understand you're looking for a long-term investment. Money no object?"

"I wouldn't say it's no object, but I'd pay above the Empress' evaluation of a business that suited me."

"If you're that interested. . . . I could pick you up tomorrow morning—"

"Late morning."

He smiled an oily smile. "Of course. Late morning. I know someone with a business she might be willing to let go, if the price is right."

"If the business is right, the price will be right. Located here in Domba?"

"Yes. A factory. The factory, actually." Chee laughed like a man trying to pretend he isn't part of what he's apologizing for. "Slave-staffed, entirely. Twelve just re-signed after the Release. There's . . . well . . . no difficulty, but. . . . It's a delicate matter." He winked.

"I know what 'delicate matter' means," I said, and didn't wink back. "I've dealt with 'delicate matters' before. I'm not afraid of 'delicate matters'."

He chuckled. "Good. Tomorrow, then."

"And make sure whatever you come to fetch me in has room for my slaves. Three of them."

"Is it really necessary—"

"Where I go, they go."

"The person you're going to see wants you to come alone."

Out of the 'phone's line of vision, Tosun slapped his chest, then Raj's, and made muscles.

"Two of them are bodyguards. I don't go anywhere without them."

"Understandable. But the third? I hear she's a. . . ."

"She was a gift from a business associate. Never mind why I keep her close, but it isn't what you think, judging by the look on your face. In fact, I ought to send my fellas—"

"Sorry—" he wiped his face clear of expression. "My mistake. You and three slaves. That won't be a problem."

"Fine. See you tomorrow."

I clicked off the 'phone.

Connie peeled away her false muzzle and rubbed her face. "At last! I don't know how you people stand these things."

Raj cocked his head. "But ours. . . ."

Connie snickered.

Raj turned to Tosun and said, "That show she's on; somebody else writes the comedy, right?"

I began to warm to the little fella.

~*~

The next day, Chee showed up just before mid-day with a closed carriage. It was drawn by half-a-dozen matched slaves — sleek fellas, all a sort of bluish-gray, all the same size and build. When Connie strutted out, they stared at her, then lowered their heads and snuck peeks.

I thought she was over-doing things a bit, but who am I to argue? She wore a typical shave-tail outfit: bright yellow plastic trousers, bright green short-sleeved shirt — it's possible she could have picked something that would have looked worse with the sapphires and pearls of her slave collar, but she had been working against time. She wore silver sunglasses with the frame of each eye shaped like a five-petaled flower, and shiny black close-toed shoes. She even stuck red-white-and-paisley scarves in the . . . you know . . . up here — where your females' lactation organs hang out all the time — excuse me, no offense, but it's . . . you know . . . alien. So she put scarves in there and let the edges show, so it would look like she was all stuffing up there, the way shave-tail females do. And you know how her hair is — all different patches? She made Tosun gather up each patch and tie a red ribbon around the end. She put gloss on her black lips. —Yes, they're really black, this was just gloss. She had gotten some false claws from somewhere, and stuck them on her fingers. She couldn't do anything with them on, but she said that was the point — she was a luxury model, she didn't have to do anything.

Chee rode inside with us, making chit-chat about the weather. He never once let his eyes rest on Connie, so maybe she was dressed right, after all.

~*~

The factory owner, Yoshe Scertz, was an overfed long-hair, brown with irregular black spots. She met us in her home, on the factory grounds. It was only two stories high, but covered with — what do you call it? — gingerbread; round towers on the front edges — no corners, of course, everything rounded.

Scertz led us into a dining room where a low table, with three pillows around it, was set for three.

"I thought we'd have a drink, to seal the bargain."

"You two," I said to Tosun and Raj. "Behind me." To Connie, I said, "Go over and inspect the factory for me. Be quick, but keep your eyes open."

"Can't that wait?" Scertz objected.

"Saves me time," I said. "If she says it's a good investment, it's a good investment. I don't even have to look."

Chee and Scertz exchanged glances. She said, "Chee, why don't you go with her? Show her around? Answer any questions she might have?"

Chee nodded.

"And Chee—" Scertz called, as he followed Connie out. He turned. "At a suitable distance, do I make myself clear? Don't touch her, don't stare at her. She is the property of my guest; treat her with respect. Respect, do you hear me?"

The Registrar nodded again, looking very sour, and left.

"I appreciate your looking out for my girl," I said to Scertz. "I didn't realize the trouble she'd cause out here in the wilds." Which was a lie, of course: Connie could cause trouble alone in a crypt. Dead.

When they got back, Connie gave me a big nod, with another nod to Raj. "Looks like a loser, and one of the slaves is just a kit, but it's perfect for what you want it for."

"Good enough," I said. "Let's do paper."

Chee fetched a stack of forms from a carved wooden chest. He laid them on the table near Scertz; she put a hand on them, her manicured claws extended. I got the message — here they were, but she wasn't ready to let them go.

"Chee told you there was . . . a special circumstance attached to this transaction," she said.

I nodded. "Something to do with the personnel, is what I gathered. Something shady with the slaves?"

Scertz's nose twitched, and her lips curled up in a tiny smile.

"It's a pleasure doing business with a man who doesn't need to have everything explained to him."

Chee shifted on his pillow, and I figured this was a not-so-subtle dig at the Registrar.

Scertz signed, I signed, I fed my credit card into her machine, got back a statement from my bank that such-and-such amount had been debited from my account, which I acknowledged; Scertz got a statement from her bank that the same amount had been credited, which she acknowledged, and the business was over.

Chee poured tall thin glasses of fermented cha for himself, Scertz, and me. He knocked his back like a pro and poured another.

"When can I take possession?" I asked.

"Next week, at the latest," Scertz answered.

Chee cut his eyes at Connie. "I'll still be in town. Available for business."

"Not now, Chee." Yoshe Scertz frowned.

"Formalities are over, aren't they?" He rose and crossed the room.

Scertz slapped the table. "Not in my house! Take it to town. Better yet, take it to Muimmea!" She turned to me and said, "He has a thing for shave-tails."

Before I could stop him, he grabbed Connie around the waist and gave her a big, slobbery lick on the nose. Licking latex — it must have tasted like the inside of a soccer ball.

Connie couldn't make a fist because of the fake claws, but she backhanded him a good one. He staggered back, almost falling over the table. I reached for him; he was too far away. He snatched Connie's hand and rubbed it, then went all the way up her arm. No fuzz, of course.

"She's not a shave-tail!"

Connie plucked off her claws, tossed them to the floor, and ripped off her muzzle. "Touch me again and see what happens."

I heard a click like I've never heard before.

Yoshe Scertz's voice was cold. "Nobody move."

Tosun said, "She has a gun."

"A what?" said Raj.

"It's a Terran weapon. Like a sling, but more deadly. Don't move."

My back hair rose. I could smell the tension in the room, and sensed my holy nephew resting at ease on his haunches.

Scertz said, "Chee, come over here." He did as he was told. "Now, we are all going to visit the factory. What bitter irony, that it should burn down just as it passed into new ownership, killing the new owner and his slaves. Here, Chee."

"She's giving him a gun," Tosun informed me; I was taking Scertz very seriously — I hadn't moved, not even my eyes.

"Stand up," Scertz said. "Chee, go in front of them. I'll bring up the rear."

Single file, we passed through the entry and out into the sunlight. Somewhere, someone had put a massive amount of fertilizer on a field. That good, fresh, clean country air.

—Yeah, that's really what I thought about. My first thought, when my brain started to work after the panic. My second thought was how I could kill Connie before Scertz and Chee got a chance. Of course, Connie would have had a point, thinking the same thing about me; after all, she wasn't the one who had called me with this mess. Then I thought how Connie and I could both kill Raj.

We were half-way to the factory when I heard a loud, fast buzz, then another, then a pair of TUNKs. Scertz sighed as she went down, but Chee collapsed without a sound.

Connie did that shriek and victory dance she does on the show when she puts one over on somebody. And from out of the bushes stepped the honeymooning couple from our bed-and-breakfast, each holding a government-issue sling.

"Shahtsi, Tosun, Raj," Connie said, "I'd like you to meet two of the Empress' finest. I called them from Tammi Resort and arranged for them to meet us in Domba. I was going to send them in to make the arrest as soon as we had the papers signed, but this is so much more satisfying, isn't it? Don't you just love the sound of justice bouncing off a skull?"

~*~

So that's what happened. I signed the factory over to Connie, she freed the bodies and sent young Jimi home — sent an armed escort to bring him to the Yolanbayt, when he was ready to try again. Some of the slaves actually offered to re-sign for her, but she wouldn't have it. Freehold or nothing, she said. She put some money into the place, and it's making a nice profit.

Raj? He should have stayed in the sticks, but he came back to Muimmea with his little brother. He wouldn't have been a bad beggar, but NOOO, he wanted a real job. Yes, he found one. Yes, he likes it. Seems to, anyway. He'll be back any minute, you can ask him yourself. So he's yellow-orange— By the Mother's grace, I don't judge people by the color of their fur. No offense.

Tiph and the Human Dilemma

When I won my contract with Premier Luxury Slaves, the first thing they did was send me to Milady's Fur — the leading salon on the planet Marner — for a makeover. Vain when I went in, I must have been insufferable when I came out, every hair gleaming and soft, from the crown of my head to the tips of my toes. They even polished my teeth, gilded my fingernails, and taught me how to keep the short hairs on my muzzle elegantly styled.

It was written into my ownership papers that anyone who bought my contract would continue to pay for me to enjoy Milady's deluxe upkeep package monthly. It was an investment, really. I mean, why spend for a luxury slave and then let her go all mangy-rangy?

Now that I was freehold, working for a non-profit, I could only afford to indulge myself in an all-day treatment once a year, for old time's sake — and, I'll admit it, because I'm still rather vain of my appearance. My mate and kits tease me about it, but gently.

Last year's visit to Milady's began with no hint of what I was about to get into. As always, the receptionist, Ahm, jumped up and circled the desk when I came in, exchanging hugs and nose-licks. "Always so good to see you, Tiph! Has it been a year already?"

"Seems like no time," I said, "and not a moment too soon."

Naturally, Ahm claimed I looked like I'd just stepped out of last year's grooming. You don't become the leading salon on the planet by telling your clientèle they need you. Neither do you send the clients straight in to their appointment; you keep them waiting just long enough to show them the latest line of fur products and accessories, then send them into their treatment room before they can buy anything. You want them to think about what they've seen while they're being pampered, so they come out in the mood to buy.

No, I'm not that clever: my boss-lady explained the psychology to me after I came back from my previous treatment loaded down with little pink bags.

My usual stylist, Krikt, had been at Milady's since before I was a client. She greeted me as warmly as Ahm had, but I thought she was a bit abstracted, although that might be what the humans call hindsight.

Not that she made any mistakes. She'd been at her profession long enough to do it on autopilot, but that wasn't how Milady's stylists did things.

I finally asked, intrusive though it was. My mate's influence, no doubt. There's never been such a man for involving himself in other people's troubles, which is lucky for me, now that I think about it.

"Is something wrong?"

Krikt put down the brush she held in now-trembling fingers. "I didn't think it showed."

"You're holding up well, but I've known you for a long time, my dear."

She sighed deeply, as if relieved to be sharing but resigned to its being a useless exercise.

"It's my oldest kit. He's been running with a mixed crowd, and it's got him . . . confused. There's this human girl. . . ."

She didn't need to say more. It wasn't the sort of thing one saw on the news, but word got around. There were humans on Marner who had been born here. As long as the children were brought up in the human neighborhoods, and taught to know their place, few Marneri had strong objections to them. But

46

when the children were allowed to mix with young Marneri, things could get uncomfortably odd.

Apparently, this was one of those times.

Krikt said, "Her name is Sylvia."

"Pretty name."

"She's pretty, for a human. She has a nose worth calling a nose and her top teeth stick out, so her face isn't as flat as most humans'. She looks almost like a young Marneri. Not really, but heading in the right direction. Still, you know: human. I mean, we love who we love, I know that, but still."

I understood her objection. Humans and Marneri were different species. True, they could be wonderful companions to each other. They were both capable of consent — you know the kind I mean — so live and let live. But they couldn't generate kits. A mother cares about that.

Krikt fiddled with a jar of fur product. "Munnin, my kit, says Sylvia plans to get facial reconstruction when she's grown and has a job. That, and full-body hair implants."

"Ugh!" It made my flesh creep, just thinking about it. My fur stood on end all over.

"I know! Between Marneri shaving all their fur and wearing clothes, and humans growing fur all over and wearing false muzzles, you hardly know who's what these days."

She was exaggerating, but not by much. My own boss-lady was a human who was sometimes mistaken for a Marneri trying to *look* human, which amused my mate and me, because she was definitely human. Opposed to slavery, and all that. Well, if you knew how the humans did slavery, you'd understand.

I smoothed the hair on my arms back down and asked, "Has she told her parents? What do they think about it all?"

Krikt shook her head, the jeweled fur-clamps below her ears catching the light. "She hasn't told them. She said they'd have a cow. That's a human word for 'objection,' apparently."

I had never come across that one before, and stored it for future use.

"I'm so sorry," I said. "Wish I could help." Easy to say, when you know there's no help to be had.

~*~

A week later, the door to our corporate office opened, and a young female human came in, dressed in a black-and-white fake-fur body suit.

I hadn't mentioned Krikt's son or his mixed-up human friend at home or at the office, knowing my mate and our employer wouldn't be able to resist getting involved. I might as well have told them, because I knew this young person was Sylvia. Just *knew* it.

She blinked, wide-eyed, when she saw me. Young ones often do.

I caught myself preening, and stopped short of running my nails through my muzzle fur. Milady's does wonderful work, and I was lucky in my looks to begin with, but I'm trying to break myself of luxury slave habits. It's hard, especially in the face of open admiration.

"Are you," she stammered, "are you Tiph Tosun?"

"I am."

She took a small step back, as if she were thinking about leaving. Then she stepped forward again and said, "My name is Sylvia Landon. My dad is Arnold Landon of Landon Imports? Munnin Gup's mother gave me your name. She said you'd help me."

I remembered having stated that empty sympathetic formula, and could have scratched a notch in my own ear. Still, a kit is a kit, whether Marneri or human, and the girl looked desperately unhappy.

"I don't know what I can do for you, dear."

"I want to be Marneri! A real Marneri! Now that I've met you, I want more than that: I want to be a *beautiful* Marneri! Like you! Show me how! Please! *Seplasas!*"

I had the strongest possible cow, but she had said "please" in Marneri. And she had touched my damnable vanity, which gave me the inspiration for what I did.

"You want to be just like me? Fine." I told her what a spa day at Milady's cost. That was my opening move. I can only assume associating with my boss-lady is training my mind into her twistiness. Sometimes I can understand that about-to-eat-somebody-else's-lunch look she gets when she thinks of a way to get what the non-profit needs from someone who doesn't want to provide it.

Sylvia's eyes widened at the price I quoted. From watching my boss-lady, I could tell she was figuring out how to get the cash or credits together.

I said, "At least once a month, preferably."

"That's impossible! You'd have to be rich!"

"I've never been rich. Far from it."

"Then how?"

"Let's take a walk."

~*~

Sylvia must have been sweltering in her full-body suit, but she chattered happily about her love of Marner and all things Marneri, about all the Marneri she'd met through her father's business and how kind they'd always been to her, how she loved the food, the music, the religions, on and on. Inevitably, she got around to cats. Cats are companion animals the humans have back home which, apparently, they think we resemble. Sometimes I think they think we *are* just big, talking cats, part pet and part God. She confirmed it when told me about some of her favorite human books about Marner.

We came to a door set into a windowless wall. I opened it and motioned her in, following her in and closing the door. "Welcome to the Slave Exchange," I said.

The courtyard was nearly empty at this time of the afternoon, most applicants having been accepted or rejected; most purchases, returns, and status changes having been registered. Afternoons were for finishing and filing the paperwork and phoning the Imperial Slavery Department.

"The what?" She might feel Marneri in her soul, but she was human enough for that one little word to stop her in her tracks.

"Slave," I repeated. "This is the slave exchange. This is how I could afford Milady's monthly. My owners paid for it. If you want to be like me—"

"You're a slave?"

"I was. My current boss bought me and registered me freehold, so I'm not a slave any more. That's why I only go to Milady's once a year now." I looked at her as if puzzled. "Didn't Munnin tell you all about slavery on Marner?" I knew he hadn't.

Humans think we don't talk about slavery because it's shameful and secret, but we don't talk about it because it's ordinary and unremarkable, generally just another career choice, strictly regulated and no more binding than any other contract. Not really slavery in the human sense of the word, but that's how they translated it into their languages, and I intended to press that for all it was worth.

I said, "I was born to a family that had once been well off but had fallen on hard times. My older siblings sold themselves into domestic service." Our "slaves" commanded signing fees, housing and board, and performance bonuses that could be more favorable than employment salaries, but I wasn't about to tell her that. "My parents said I had the looks to try for luxury slave, so I auditioned for it and won a contract."

Her bare skin turned that pasty color humans get when they're shocked. "What did. . . . What did you have to do?"

"Whatever I was told." I couldn't be told to do anything other than stand around and look as decorative as possible, to be ostentatiously useless, to indicate that the owner of my registration papers was rich enough to afford a luxury slave. Again, I wasn't about to tell Sylvia that.

"But Munnin's family don't have slaves."

"Then at least some of Munnin's family *are* slaves. Ask him."

She backed up. "Let's go."

"We haven't been inside yet. I want to show you the room I lived in while I waited for my contract to be picked up. If you have yourself declared fully Marneri, you could audition for luxury slave, like I did. You might even have my same room."

"No. Please. I want to go home."

"Don't be frightened. We're perfectly safe." I had my freehold papers in my waist pouch, which was probably where Sylvia carried hers. She did carry hers, didn't she? Surely, she carried hers. I would never have brought her into the slave exchange if I hadn't been certain she carried her freehold papers.

A tall, scrawny male, orange, with pale orange stripes, stepped between us, facing Sylvia. He wrapped a hand around her upper arm and grinned toothily at me over his shoulder.

"Claim!"

Sylvia tried to pull away from him, but he gripped her, using his nails to discourage struggle.

I put a hand on his shoulder — a trembling hand, I have no doubt.

"You don't understand," I said. "She's human."

He looked at Sylvia more closely, and laughed. "So she is!" He used one long finger to peel up the fur on her head, exposing the human hair beneath.

"Let me go!" Sylvia reached into her waist pouch, and I relaxed until she pulled out a student ID. "My dad is Arnold Landon of Landon Imports."

"Is he, now? Well, I'm thinking that Arnold Landon of Landon Imports might pay more than you're worth to buy you freehold."

"She's already freehold. You know she is. Humans are registered freehold at birth or as soon as they land." Desperately, I said, "Sylvia, show him your papers. Show him, dear."

Her voice rose to a wail that hurt my ears. The way Sylvia's claimant's ears pulled back, it seemed to hurt his, too. I wondered if Munnin had ever heard that noise.

"I don't carry that silly thing! Everybody knows humans are free!"

The slaver placed his palm over Sylvia's face, spreading his fingers so she could look through and see his expression.

"Hush," he said. "Humans who go out without their papers are only free until they get caught. But don't worry. Daddy will be happy to pay."

I was in SO MUCH TROUBLE! Yes, her father would pay, and she would be scolded and possibly disciplined (assuming humans discipline their children which, from their behavior, I rather doubt). But I was the one who put her in this predicament by not checking her papers before I brought her to the exchange. And me, an employee of a non-profit dedicated to rescuing slaves from abusive relationships!

Ah!

"No," I said, as firmly as if I were talking to one of my own kits.

He turned around, keeping his grip on Sylvia. "Excuse me?"

"I said no." Slowly, I reached into my waist pouch (where my freehold papers rested securely) and pulled out one of my business cards. I handed it to the man, keeping my thumb over it until he held the card, so the name of our organization hit him all at once.

I kept a straight face when he looked from the card to me to the card to me again.

"You may have heard of us," I said. "Have we heard of you?"

He decided to bluster. "Look, I'm within my rights, here."

Then I said those three little words my boss-lady has used to reduce many a miscreant to jelly: "What's your name?"

He released the card and Sylvia, holding his empty hands up and open.

"I don't want any trouble," he said.

I still kept my face impassive and said, "Too late."

"Traitor!" he said, backing toward the exchange building. "Troublemaker! *Human-lover*!"

I thrust my face toward him, wrinkled my nose, and bared my teeth up to the gums. I don't know what I would have done if he'd accepted the fight challenge, but I was right in guessing he'd lower his head and continue to back away.

I reached out for Sylvia.

"Take my hand, and don't let go until we get back to the office, you silly girl! I can give you temporary freehold papers until you get home. And don't come out without your papers ever again, do you hear me, young lady?"

She gulped and nodded. "Thank you, Tiph. I'll never forget this."

"By the way," I said, "when you're ready for those operations Krikt tells me you want, let me know and I'll recommend a good practitioner."

"No thanks! I mean, thank you, but I don't think I'll do that after all."

~*~

I didn't reproach Krikt for sending Sylvia to me when she called to thank me. A mother will stop at nothing for her kit; I certainly understand that.

She said, "Munnin is still friends with that girl, but she doesn't want to be a Marneri anymore, and she argues with him about *slavery*, of all things."

"That's humans for you," I said.

I don't know what Sylvia told her father, but I do know my boss-lady went hopping around the office waving a credit transfer from him, saying he had made a monthly pledge to our organization.

I had almost forgotten the incident when my boss-lady came into my office with a human female in her wake.

"We have a new volunteer," she said. "She'll be under your direction to begin with. She's very eager to help us. She says you've met." She went into her office and left us together.

It was Sylvia. I hadn't recognized her in her human skin and those cloth coverings they wear in place of natural fur.

Sylvia stared after the boss-lady. She sighed.

"Isn't she wonderful?" she said. "I want to be just like her."

The Old School Tie

Me, Cornelia Phelan from Hell Alley, with a Threedy on my mantelpiece.

It hadn't happened yet, but I had just finished doing the lead voice on that animated biopic about the life of Bette Midler, the one that made her a household name again. It broke me out of being "just" a comedienne and shoved me up the acting hierarchy from zany laff riot into the ranks of critical respectability.

The PR department had been working overtime, leaking clips to entertainment news outlets and generating buzz about a sure nomination and possible win (I won) at the 3D Awards.

They wanted me to go back to Earth to do a publicity tour, but I had succeeded in convincing them to shoot the pic on the planet Marner, where I live now, and I succeeded in convincing them it would be more effective for me to do the publicity from here, too.

It isn't like anybody back on Earth cares about meeting celebrities in person anymore. Holograms are almost as lifelike as real people, they don't choke you with too much perfume, and you can turn them off when you're done. You can share the publicity experience with thousands of your fellow fans, each from the comfort of home. No parking hassle, no traffic, nobody picking your pocket or barfing on your shoes.

Marneri, on the other hand, love the in-the-flesh fellowship that the cool human kids (the ones on Earth and some of the ones residing on Marner) call *meat-ings*.

So I wasn't surprised when, after my first publicity broadcast, I walked down the street to calls of *Connie!* and

Bette Midler! And, in Marneri, *Wind beneath my wings!* I wasn't surprised when Marneri fans came up to me and shook my hand to show me they knew human customs; some of them put a hand over their mouth to demonstrate they had no intention of licking my nose, which is how Marneri greet each other.

What disoriented me was when a woman called, in a thin, uncertain voice, in a tone that hoped to be heard but didn't want to intrude, "Connie-o?"

I looked for who had called that name I hadn't heard for umpty-ump years, and the fan who had just finished telling me that roses don't grow from seed swiveled her ears, turned, and pointed to the source.

In case you couldn't guess, I was a loner in school, with an attitude that waved a flag and dared anybody to *try* adjusting it. I made people mad and I made people laugh, but I didn't make friends.

There was one exception: one of the middle-class kids, one of the few kids who ever gave me the time of day.

And now, on a street on another planet, she stood before me, a big smile on her face. She held her arms away from her body but not quite extended, signaling an openness to a hug but not an entitlement.

To be honest, I had forgotten her existence. For twenty years, I had been so focused on poking a finger in the eye of the snobs who had shut me out, I had forgotten the girls who had been buddies since first grade but had opened their clique to me when my Aunt Bootsie had taken me in and transferred me to Day High.

Even though most childhood memories generally triggered a full load of poison, I hugged her, with a couple of long-time-no-see pats on the back for good measure.

"I'm Beth," she said. "You probably don't remember me. I know who you are, of course! I mean, I'd remember you anyway, but e-EV-rybody knows you now!"

"Of course I remember you!" And how *could* I have forgotten? How *could* I? Details sprang out like holograms from a pop-up book. "You and Jane and Kathie and Paula and I used to play That's What *She* Said in the halls."

Beth threw back her head and guffawed, one of the things I had always liked best about her. "Oh, Connie-o, you take me back to my youth!"

I grinned. "That's what *she* said."

She gave a rich, deep chuckle. "We were such dorks!"

That made me laugh. Beth had picked up a boatload of slang from her great-grandfather, who passed it on from his grandfather, and she had shared it with anybody who wanted it. I had forgotten it as soon as I left school, but it came rushing back to me now. I needed to record all of it I could remember and work it into my next series for TerraNet, currently under development.

"So are you on vacation or living here?" I asked.

"Living. I couldn't afford to be here for fun." That was another thing I liked about Beth: no pretension, no bullshit. "I married a geologist, and he took a transfer here with a promotion and a raise. Our kids are all here, so we up and came!"

"Do you have some time? Would you like some tea or something?"

"I do, and I would."

I snagged a passerby heading in the right direction and said, in Marneri, "I need to get a message to Tell It To The Empress headquarters. Tell them I'm doing a thing, and I'll get there when I get there. *Seplases*?" The first thing I learned about Marner is the importance of saying please. My Aunt Bootsie would have told me I should have learned that on Earth, and years earlier.

The passerby nodded and licked my nose. Then he touched the tip of it, indicating he didn't expect a lick in return. I'd have preferred a handshake, but a lick and a pass was the next best thing.

My favorite hole-in-the-wall noodle joint was right down the street, so I hustled Beth in there before any more fans could waylay me. The last thing I wanted at this uncharacteristically heartwarming moment was a gibbering fanboy with my name shaved into his back fur in Marneri script.

Beth followed me past an admittedly sketchy exterior, without a sound or a second's hesitation, and I remembered what a sport she was. Middle-class, like I said, and personally fastidious, but she'd sort night-crawlers with a night-crawler sorter if she found herself in company with one.

I ordered a light snack of cold noodles and vegetables and the native infusion we humans christened "tea". Beth ordered the same.

She openly gazed around at the native décor and the Marneri script on the menu, remarking on how beautiful and different everything was. I was surprised when she read the restaurant's motto, which was only written in Marneri: *We Make Everything Lickable.*

She looked up and smiled. "Johnny's company offered a course in written and spoken Marneri, and we took it. It seemed stupid to come here without knowing how to communicate."

Most humans don't worry about that; they live in what they call Little Earth, but tolerance of the Other seemed typical of Beth. She had befriended *me*, after all.

Our food and tea came.

I asked, "So where is everybody? The old high school crew?" Before today, I would have said that I asked just to be asking, that I didn't really care, but I did. I did care. I cared so much, it almost ticked me off.

She filled me in. They had all had moderate-to-great success, but Beth finished each happy story with, "Nothing like what *you've* done, of course," as if I'd be jealous of my friends. The only triumphs I'm bitter about are the ones of the high-rise snots who made everybody's lives miserable in school and beyond.

A kit shuffled up to the table, head lowered but cocked up sideways to gauge my reaction to its approach. *Her* approach, I corrected myself, when I noticed the fur clip on the top of her head. I looked beyond her, to see beaming parents at a nearby table.

I greeted her in Marneri. She giggled and returned the greeting.

Just when I thought all she was going to do was stare and giggle, she took a deep breath and quavered the theme song from the series I'd just wrapped up.

Beth and I applauded, and the other patrons joined in. The kit put her hands over her muzzle and groomed it; she was so nervous and pleased, the fur must have been standing out hard enough to tickle.

I thanked her, and she ran back and buried her face in her mother's side.

When the waitress came to see if we wanted anything else, I told her to put the kit's family's order on my bill. It's these little attentions that boost popularity.

Something was nagging at me, and it finally dropped.

"You didn't mention Paula. Don't tell me she's passed." By which I meant "died". Sometimes my Aunt Bootsie rises up in me and one of her expressions comes out of my mouth.

Beth said, "No, she's alive. I just didn't want to be a Debbie Downer. Paula's had a bad time of it. She married a boy from Morrisette High."

"No! Traitor!" Morrisette was our traditional football rival.

Beth used another of her grandfather's slangy sayings: "I know, right? No, they had a good marriage. I mean, they still do, but he lost his job last year and he's really depressed about it. They're here on Marner."

"What is this, Day High in the sky?"

She didn't laugh. "That's the worst part. Not being here, obviously, but that they moved here for Michael's work, since

Paula can get a good job anywhere — She's a vascular surgeon — but then Michael got cut when the company downsized."

If there's one thing I know, it's Marneri law. "The company has to move them back."

"They don't want to go back. They like it here."

I was, frankly, pretty tired of Earth people migrating to Marner. It was a physically beautiful planet with most of it still natural, and I wanted to see it stay that way. Needless to say, *I* wanted to stay, and, yes, I realize how hypocritical that is. Sue me.

I gestured for the check.

Beth said, "Michael's always been a good cook, so he started a catering business, but it's hard. Paula's pretty much supporting it, and Michael is worried they're throwing good money after bad. Michael's like me: We both get snappish when we're stressed, and Paula isn't very patient with being snapped at. I don't know what's going to become of them."

I was about to say *Life is tough,* but I noticed the kit and her family standing at my elbow, waiting to thank me and listening to Paula and Michael's sad, sad story.

"What's the name of this catering business?" I asked.

"Michael's catering business?"

No, I thought, *Bette Midler's catering business.* But I said, "Yes."

"Michael's Catering."

"Yes, Michael's catering. What's its name?"

"That's the name: Michael's Catering."

I quoted the mock motto the Day High kids had made up for our rival school: "Morrisette — We brain good."

Beth snickered along with me. That's what I like: a basically nice person with a healthy snide streak.

"Hey, you know what?" I said. "Let's call him!"

"Now?"

"Right now. We'll go to my office and see what we can do."

The kit and her parents glowed with delight at overhearing Connie Phelan being generous. Yeah, generous: I was dropping the worm of privilege into the sea of need, fishing for admiration and gratitude. Sometimes I turn my own stomach.

~*~

It wasn't far to the office, but I hired a rickshaw so I could avoid my fans. Even so, I had to wave like a Prom Queen now and then.

Tell It To The Empress, my NGO, is staffed by three full-time employees (all Marneri), a varying number of volunteers, and sometimes myself. We investigate reported and suspected violations of Marneri slave law that slips through the cracks of the Empress's regulators. It's fun. I've nearly been Shanghaied myself, so it's also personal.

We had just busted an underground sweatshop, and Beth and I had to run a gauntlet of grateful releasees and their relatives. I don't know if I was more puffed up with pride or filled with self-loathing for being proud of bankrolling something I could well afford.

Before I closed Beth into my office with me, I asked my right-hand gal, Tiph Tosun, to get Michael's Catering on the phone for me.

I poured myself a gin and tonic and Beth a ginger ale before the intercom told me Tiph had Michael on the line.

I introduced myself as a friend of his wife and asked if he could cater a high-end mixed human/Marneri dinner to mark the twenty-fifth anniversary of the accession of the Empress. On the spur of the moment, I asked if he could manage a quick-and-simple pop-up celebration at Tell It To The Empress right now.

He gave a short laugh and said, "That, I can do. The dinner party, probably not. I hate to turn down a friend of Paula's but it's either feast or famine, you know? An hour ago, I would have killed for a job. Then a Marneri couple called and hired me to do a birthday bash for their little girl, and it's been one call after another since then. This afternoon is the last free day I'll have for two months. Crazy, isn't it?"

I agreed it was crazy, and transferred him to Tiph to coordinate buying and delivering supplies. While I was at it, I had her announce the imminent festivities on the premises.

Beth's jaw dropped in exaggerated surprise when I told her Michael's good news. Then she pointed at me and said, "You did this!"

"How? I just called him this minute."

"Yes, but you made me tell you the name of his business in front of that couple and their little fan-girl. You knew they would hire him for something, or spread the word about Connie Phelan wanting him to have work."

It had never occurred to me, and I said so.

True to form, Beth opened her mouth and the truth fell out. "You were never modest in high school."

"I'm still not," I said.

She narrowed her eyes. "Uh-huh."

I flapped a hand at her. "Whatever. Stay for the party?"

"I'd love to."

"Call your family. See if they can come. The more the merrier."

"And we can spread the word about the good work you do here. Clever girl!"

"Modest and clever," I said. "*God*, what a paragon."

Beth swirled the ice in her ginger ale and smirked. "That's what *she* said."

About The Author

Marian Allen was born in Louisville, Kentucky and now lives in rural Indiana. For as long as she can remember, she's loved telling and being told stories. When, at the age of about six, she was informed that somebody got paid for writing all those books and movies and television shows, she abandoned her previous ambition (beachcomber), and became a writer.

She's worked as a high school teacher, an executive secretary, a soda jerk, a bank clerk, an accountant, and in Red Cross Youth Services.

She likes connecting and reconnecting with people, meeting new friends and keeping in touch with the friends she already has.

Her writing reflects her love of network. In her books and stories, no one exists in total isolation, but in a web of connections to family, friends, colleagues, self at former stages of maturity, perceptions, and self-images. Most of her work is fantasy, science fiction and/or mystery, though she writes horror, humor, romance, mainstream, or anything else that suits the story and characters.

If you enjoyed this book, please consider buying other titles by this author. Excerpts, blog posts, free stories, and buy links to various formats are available at:

Marian Allen, Author Lady - Fantasies, mysteries, comedies, recipes
http://MarianAllen.com

www.ingramcontent.com/pod-product-compliance
Lightning Source LLC
Chambersburg PA
CBHW072044170626
46811CB00008B/3157